Maths Together

There's a lot more to maths than numbers and sur
it's an important language which helps us describe, explore and
explain the world we live in. So the earlier children develop
an appreciation and understanding of maths, the better.

We use maths all the time – when we shop or travel from one
place to another, for example. Even when we fill the kettle we are
estimating and judging quantities. Many games and puzzles
involve maths. So too do stories and poems, often
in an imaginative and interesting way.

Maths Together is a collection of high-quality picture books
designed to introduce children, simply and enjoyably, to basic
mathematical ideas – from counting and measuring to pattern and
probability. By listening to the stories and rhymes, talking about
them and asking questions, children will gain the confidence to try
out the mathematical ideas for themselves – an important step
in their numeracy development.

You don't have to be a mathematician to help your child
learn maths. Just as by reading aloud you play a vital role in their
literacy development, so by sharing the *Maths Together* books
with your child, you will play an important part in developing their
understanding of mathematics. To help you, each book has detailed
notes at the back, explaining the mathematical ideas that it
introduces, with suggestions for further related activities.

With *Maths Together*, you can count on doing the
very best for your child.

For my parents, with love
R. M.

First published 1999 by Walker Books Ltd
87 Vauxhall Walk, London SE11 5HJ

2 4 6 8 10 9 7 5 3 1

Text © 1999 Clare Boucher
Illustrations © 1999 Rachel Merriman
Introductory and concluding notes
© 1999 Jeannie Billington and Grace Cook

This book has been typeset in Fontesque.

Printed in Singapore

British Library Cataloguing in Publication Data
A catalogue record for this book is
available from the British Library.

ISBN 0-7445-6836-6 (hb)
ISBN 0-7445-6807-2 (pb)

THE SIX BLIND MEN AND THE ELEPHANT

A Traditional Indian Story

Retold by Clare Boucher

Illustrated by Rachel Merriman

WALKER BOOKS

AND SUBSIDIARIES

LONDON · BOSTON · SYDNEY

In a village by a river in India lived six blind men. They could not see, but they could touch and feel and hear and talk. In the heat of the day they sat beneath a neem tree and talked of many things.

One day a little boy
ran through the village shouting,
"There's an elephant
down by the river!"
"Ah, an elephant,"
said Haresh.

"I wonder," said Nimish,
"if it is a big or a small elephant."
"An elephant," said Vinod. "What **is** an elephant?"
"An elephant is ... well, I don't know," said Sunil.
"What is an elephant **like**?" said Hiran.
"I'm sure I don't know," said Pran.
In fact, none of them knew.
So the six blind men went down to the
river to find out what an elephant is like.

Haresh touched the elephant.
He could not see it,
but he could feel it.
He felt its trunk.
"Ah," he said, "now I know
what an elephant is like.
It is like a snake.
It is long and rubbery."

Nimish touched the elephant.
He could not see it, but he could feel it.
He felt its tusks.
"Oh," he said, "now I know what
an elephant is like. It is like a knife.
It is sharp and cold."

Vinod touched the elephant.
He could not see it, but he could feel it.
He felt its ear.
"Hmm," he said, "now I know what
an elephant is like. It is like a big leaf.
It is smooth and flat."

Sunil touched the elephant.
He could not see it,
but he could feel it.
He felt its leg.
"Ahh," he said, "now I know what
an elephant is like. It is like a tree.
It is round and hard."

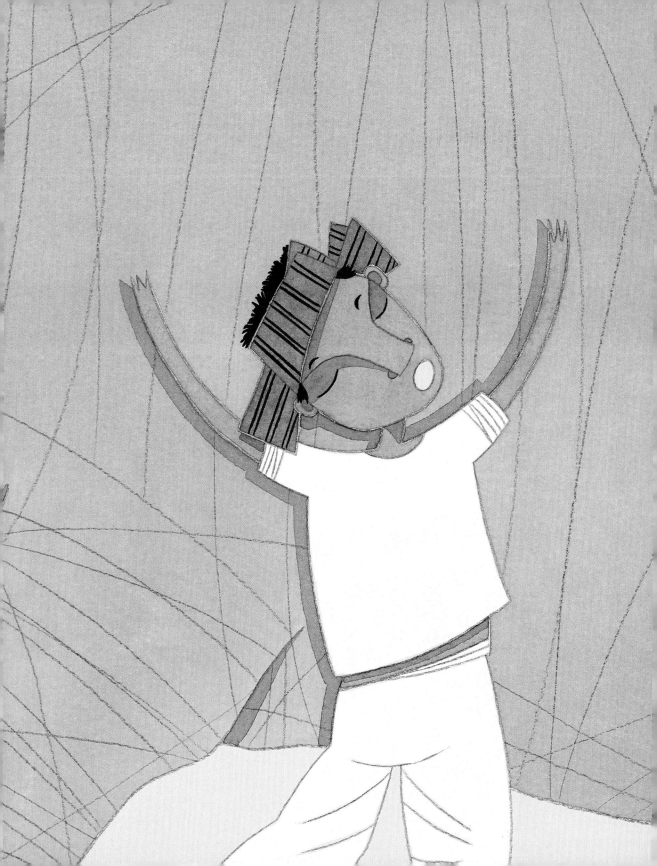

Hiran touched the elephant.
He could not see it,
but he could feel it.
He felt its side.
"Ah-ha," he said, "now I know
what an elephant is like.
It is like a wall.
It is high and wide."

Pran touched the elephant.
He could not see it, but he could feel it.
He felt its tail.
"Yes," he said, "now I know what
an elephant is like.
It is like a rope.
It is long and thin."

"An elephant," said Haresh, "is long and rubbery like a snake."

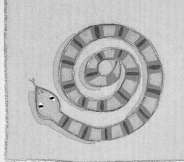

"It is sharp and cold like a knife," said Nimish.

"It is smooth and flat like a leaf," said Vinod.

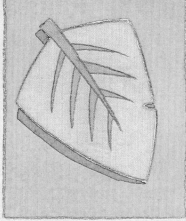

"It is round and hard like a tree," said Sunil.

"It is high and wide like a wall," said Hiran.

"It is long and thin like a rope," said Pran.

And the six blind men began to
shout at one another.
"NO, NO, NO...
I AM RIGHT AND
YOU ARE WRONG!"

"Excuse me!"
said a big, soft voice...

"None of you are wrong,"
said the elephant.
"You are **all** right.
My trunk is like a snake,
my tusks are like knives,
my ears are like leaves,
my legs are like trees,
my sides are like walls,
and my tail is like a rope."

"Oh!" said the six blind men.

"Long and rubbery…"
said Haresh.
"Sharp and cold…"
said Nimish.
"Smooth and flat…"
said Vinod.
"Round and hard…"
said Sunil.

"High and wide…"
said Hiran.
"Long and thin…"
said Pran.

"That," laughed the
six blind men, "is what
an elephant is like!"

About this book

The story of the six blind men's efforts to find out
what an elephant is introduces children to an important part
of maths – reasoning; that is, trying to solve problems
and being able to explain your thinking.

The blind men decide to feel an elephant to find out
what it is. Based on what they have felt, they describe
what they think an elephant is like, and give their
reasons, coming to very different conclusions.
Although none of them are wrong, each man has only
felt a part of the whole. Together, they do know
what an elephant is like.

Giving reasons and sharing explanations is something
children have to learn to do for themselves. It's a bit like
learning to walk – you can watch, support, advise and
encourage children, and you *need* to do this, but you
can't do the walking for them.

Later on, children learn to reason in more mathematical
ways, using prediction, generalization and proof.

Notes for parents

Each of the six blind men in the story compares the elephant to something different. You can encourage your child to think of other comparisons too.

What else is smooth and flat?

The top of the table…?

Talking together about the story gives children the chance to tell you about the book and ask questions.

Who was right?

They all were.

"What do you think of…?" is a game children can play with you or with their friends. One person thinks of something – it could be an everyday object (e.g. a teapot) or a mathematical concept (e.g. a square, a number) – and the others say what the word brings to mind. This game is about how people see things, not about being right or wrong.

What do you think of when I say six?

It's nearly my age.

It's seven take away one.

It's the number in our family – with Jack!

t's hard and nooth … and it's round.

A marble?

You can play the "feely bag" game together too. Make a collection of things which all feel different – a rubber ball, an orange, soap, a shell, a silk handkerchief. Put them in a bag. One person puts their hand in the bag, feels one of the objects and then describes it. The others try and guess what it is.

Asking children questions can help them think more clearly. It's important to ask lots of different kinds: questions that have one right answer (e.g. What is 7 add 5?), questions that have a variety of possible answers (e.g. How many ways can you make 10 with two numbers?), and questions, like those below, that give your child the chance to predict, compare and explain things.

You can play two games using the elephants on the opposite page.
In the first, one person chooses an elephant and gives the others clues to help them guess which it is (e.g. "It's squirting, it's small and it's yellow"). To play the second game, which is more difficult, close the book. One person chooses an elephant and this time the others have to ask questions to find out which it is.

The elephant game

Maths Together

The *Maths Together* programme is divided into two sets – yellow (age 3+) and green (age 5+). There are six books in each set, helping children learn maths through story, rhyme, games and puzzles.

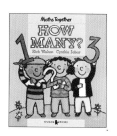
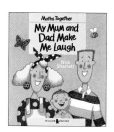

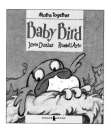

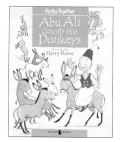
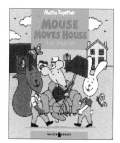